Disney's
THE LITTLE
MERMAID

Parragon
Bath • New York • Singapore • Hong Kong • Cologne • Delhi • Melbourne

This book belongs to

| | |
|---|---|
| Narrator | Roy Dotrice |
| Ariel | Jodi Benson |
| Flounder | Jason Marin |
| Scuttle | Buddy Hackett |
| Sir Grimsby | Ben Wright |
| Eric | Christopher Barnes |
| Ursula | Pat Carroll |
| Sebastian | Samuel E. Wright |
| Triton | Kenneth Mars |
| Eels (Flotsam and Jetsam) | Paddi Edwards |

Produced by Ted Kryczko and Randy Thornton
Engineered by George Charouhas

Under the Sea (02:17)
Music by Alan Menken
Lyrics by Howard Ashman
Performed by Samuel E. Wright


This is a Parragon book
This edition published by Parragon in 2009
Parragon
Queen Street House
4 Queen Street
Bath, BA1 1HE, UK

ISBN 978-1-4075-6135-6
Printed in China

Once upon a time, a little mermaid named Ariel frolicked below the ocean, exploring the hulls of sunken ships. She beckoned to her playmate, a roly-poly fish. "Come on, Flounder! I'm sure this old boat has lots of human treasure aboard."

"I'm not g-g-going in there! It's spooky."

"Don't be such a guppy! Follow me!" Swimming inside the ship's cabin, Ariel discovered some rusted silverware. "Oh, my gosh! Have you ever seen anything so wonderful?"

Ariel swam to the water's surface and found her seagull friend. "Scuttle, do you know what this is?" She held up the fork.

"Judging from my expert knowledge of humans ... it's obviously a ... a dingelhopper! Humans use these to straighten their hair!"

"Thanks, Scuttle! It's perfect for my collection." Ariel dove to an undersea grotto, where she kept her treasures from the human world. She hid her collection there because her father, the Sea King, forbade merpeople to have any contact with humans.

That night, Ariel saw strange lights shimmering over the ocean and swam up to investigate.

On the surface, she gaped at fireworks that flared above a large sailing ship. Scuttle soared down through the flickering colours. "Some celebration, huh, sweetie? It's the birthday of the human they call Prince Eric."

Forgetting her father's decree, Ariel peered at the young man on deck. "I've never seen a human this close. He's very handsome."

Aboard the ship, Eric's advisor, Sir Grimsby, motioned for the crew's attention. "It is now my privilege to present our esteemed prince with a very expensive, very large birthday gift – a marble statue carved in his exact likeness! Of course, I had hoped it would be a wedding present."

The prince glanced away, gazing at the sea. "Don't start, Grim. The right girl's out there ... somewhere."

Far beneath the ocean, the wicked Sea Witch, Ursula, used her magic to spy on Ariel. "My, my. The daughter of the great Sea King, Triton, in love with a human! A prince, no less. Her daddy will love that! Serves him right, that miserable old tyrant! Banishing me from his palace, just because I was a little ambitious.

"Still, this headstrong, lovesick girl may be the key to my revenge on Triton. She'll be the perfect bait – when I go fishing for her father!"

On the surface, a sudden storm whipped across the ocean. The prince took charge. "Stand fast! Secure the rigging!"

Without warning, a huge bolt of lightning struck the vessel. Sir Grimsby slid across the deck. "Eric, look out! The mast is falling!"

Ariel watched in horror. "Eric's been knocked into the water! I've got to save him!"

With the storm swirling about her, Ariel desperately searched for Eric. "Where is he? If I don't find him soon – wait, there he is!"

Diving beneath the waves, Ariel spotted the unconscious figure. "He's sinking fast! I've got to pull him out of the water before he drowns!" She took hold of Eric and, using all her strength, managed to drag him to the surface.

As the storm died down, Ariel dragged the unconscious prince to shore. "He's still breathing! He must be alive."

A Jamaican crab scuttled across the sand. It was Sebastian, the Sea King's music director. "Ariel, get away from dat human! Your father forbids contact with dem, remember?"

"But Sebastian, why can't I stay with him? Why can't I be part of his world?" And she sang a haunting melody that voiced her longing to be with Eric forever.

A moment later, Ariel was back in the water, and Sir Grimsby was kneeling beside Eric. "You really delight in these sadistic strains on my blood pressure, don't you?"

"Grim, a girl rescued me … She was singing in the most beautiful voice …"

"I think you've swallowed a bit too much seawater! Here, Eric, let me help you to your feet."

Back at the coral palace, Triton noticed Ariel floating about as if in a dream. Summoning Sebastian, the Sea King smiled. "You've been keeping something from me. I can tell Ariel's in love."

"I tried to stop her! I told her to stay away from humans!"

"Humans! Ariel is in love with a human?"

Triton found Ariel in her grotto. She was staring at Eric's statue, which Flounder had retrieved after the storm. "How many times have I told you to stay away from those fish-eating barbarians! Humans are dangerous!"

"But, Daddy, I love Eric!"

"So help me, Ariel, I am going to get through to you no matter what it takes!" Raising his trident, the Sea King destroyed all her treasures. Then he stormed off, leaving Ariel in tears.

As she wept, two eels slithered up to her. "Don't be ssscared. We represent sssomeone who can help you!"

Ariel followed them to Ursula's den. "My dear, sweet child! I haven't seen you since your father banished me from his court! To show that I've reformed, I'll grant you three days as a human to win your prince. Before sunset on the third day, you must get him to kiss you. If you do, he's yours forever. But if you don't – you'll be mine!"

Ariel took a deep breath and nodded. The Sea Witch smiled deviously. "Oh yes, I almost forgot. We haven't discussed payment. I'm not asking much. All I want is – your voice!"

Sebastian, who had followed Ariel, scurried out of hiding. "Don't listen, Ariel! She is a demon!" But Ursula had already used her powers to capture Ariel's beautiful voice in a seashell – and transform the little mermaid into a human!

Aided by Sebastian and Flounder, Ariel used her new legs to swim awkwardly to shore. There she found Prince Eric walking his dog. "Down, Max, down! I'm awfully sorry, miss."

Eric studied Ariel as she shied away from the animal. "Hey, wait a minute. Don't I know you? Have ... have we ever met?"

Ariel opened her mouth to answer, forgetting that her voice was gone. The prince lowered his eyes. "You can't speak or sing, either? Then I guess we haven't met."

Eric gently took Ariel's arm. "Well, the least I can do is make amends for my dog's bad manners. C'mon, I'll take you to the palace and get you cleaned up."

At the royal estate, Ariel was whisked upstairs by a maid. Grimsby discovered the prince staring glumly out the window. "Eric, be reasonable! Young ladies don't go around rescuing people, then disappearing into thin air!"

"I'm telling you, she was real! If only I could find her ..."

The following afternoon, Eric took Ariel for a rowboat ride across a lagoon. Sebastian swam below them. "Almost two days gone and dat boy hasn't puckered up once! How she gonna get dat boy to kiss her? Maybe dis will help create de romantic mood."

He began conducting a sea-creature chorus. "C'mon and kiss de girl ... The music's working! Eric's leaning over to kiss Ariel." As the prince bent toward her, the boat tipped and both Eric and Ariel fell into the water!

From her ocean lair, Ursula saw them tumble into the lagoon. "That was too close for comfort! I can't let Ariel get away that easily!"

She began concocting a magic potion. "Soon Triton's daughter will be mine! Then I'll make the Sea King writhe and wriggle like a worm on a hook!"

The next morning, Scuttle flew into Ariel's room to congratulate her. The prince had announced his wedding!

Overjoyed at the news, Ariel hurried downstairs. She hid when she saw Eric introducing Grimsby to a mysterious dark-haired maiden. The prince seemed hypnotized. "Vanessa saved my life. We're going to be married on board ship at sunset."

Ariel drew back, confused. She was the one who had rescued Eric! Fighting tears, she fled the palace.

Sebastian found Ariel sitting on the dock, watching the wedding ship leave the harbour.

Suddenly, Scuttle crash-landed beside them. "When I flew over the boat, I saw Vanessa's reflection in a mirror! She's the Sea Witch – in disguise! And she's wearing the seashell containing Ariel's voice. We've got to stop the wedding!"

Sebastian splashed into the water. "Flounder, you help Ariel swim out to dat boat! I'm going to get de Sea King!"

Dripping wet, Ariel climbed aboard the ship just before sunset, as Eric and the maiden were about to be married.

Before Vanessa could say "I do", Scuttle and an army of his friends attacked her. In the scuffle, the maiden's seashell necklace crashed to the deck, freeing Ariel's voice. Suddenly, Vanessa sounded like the Sea Witch. "Eric, get away from her!"

Ariel smiled at the prince. "Oh Eric, I wanted to tell you …"

Ursula grinned. "You're too late! The sun has set!"

Ariel felt her body changing back into a mermaid. As she dove into the water, the witch transformed her into a helpless sea plant. "You're mine, angelfish! But don't worry – you're merely the bait to catch your father! Why, here he is now!"

"I'll make a deal with you, Ursula – just don't harm my daughter!"

Instantly, Triton was changed into a tiny plant, and Ariel resumed her mermaid form. She stood heartbroken before Ursula, now Queen of the Ocean.

Suddenly, Prince Eric appeared. He tossed a harpoon at the Sea Witch, hitting her in the arm. Ursula snatched up the king's trident. "You little fool!"

As the Sea Witch pointed the weapon at Eric, Ariel rammed into her, knocking the trident loose. "Eric, we have to get away from here!"

The moment they surfaced, huge tentacles shot out of the ocean. "Eric, we're surrounded. Look out!"

Ariel gasped as an enormous monster emerged. It was the Sea Witch! Using her new powers, the witch commanded the waters into a deadly whirlpool. Several old sunken ships rose to the surface.

The prince struggled aboard one of the boats. As Ursula loomed above Ariel, Eric plunged the sharp prow through the Sea Witch, destroying her. The mighty force sent Eric reeling toward shore.

As the unconscious prince lay on the beach, Ariel perched on a rock and gazed at him. Triton and Sebastian watched from afar. "She really does love him, doesn't she, Sebastian?" The Sea King waved his trident, and Ariel was once again human.

The next day, she and Prince Eric were married on board the wedding ship. As they kissed, the humans and merpeople sent up a happy cheer, linked at last by the marriage of two people whose love was as deep as the sea and as pure as a young girl's voice.

Bath • New York • Singapore • Hong Kong • Cologne • Delhi • Melbourne

This book belongs to

| Characters (in order of appearance) | |
|---|---|
| Narrator | Mary D'Arcy |
| The Queen | Eda Reiss Merin |
| The Prince | Jerry Whitman |
| Magic Mirror | Tony Jay |
| The Huntsman | Peter Renaday |
| Snow White | Mary Kay Bergman |
| Doc | Hal Smith |
| Grumpy | Corey Burton |

Adapted by Randy Thornton
Produced by Randy Thornton and Ted Kryczko
Engineered by George Charouhas
Heigh-Ho (01:09)
Words by Larry Morey and Music by Frank Churchill
Perfomed by the Dwarf Chorus


This edition published by Parragon in 2009
Parragon
Queen Street House
4 Queen Street
Bath BA1 1HE, UK



ISBN 978-1-4075-6137-0

Manufactured in China

Once upon a time, there lived a lovely little princess named Snow White. Her vain and wicked stepmother, the Queen, feared that one day Snow White's beauty would surpass her own. So she dressed the little princess in rags and forced her to work as a servant in the castle.

Each day, the Queen consulted her magic mirror. "Magic Mirror on the wall, who is the fairest one of all?"

As long as the mirror responded in the Queen's favour, Snow White was safe.

One day, as Snow White was drawing water from a well, she made a wish. She wished that the one she loved would find her, and she dreamed about how nice he would be.

As she gazed into the wishing well, she saw another face reflected in the water. It belonged to a handsome prince. "Hello. Did I frighten you? Please don't run away!"

But the startled princess had fled to her balcony, where she could watch him from afar.

At that moment, the Queen was spying on Snow White and the Prince. When she saw them together, she flew into a jealous rage and rushed to her magic mirror, demanding an answer.

"Famed is thy beauty, Majesty, but hold! A lovely maid I see. Rags cannot hide her gentle grace. She is more fair than thee."

"Alas for her! Reveal her name."

"Lips red as a rose, hair black as ebony, skin white as snow ..."

"SNOW WHITE!"

Furious, the Queen sent for her huntsman. "Take Snow White far into the forest. Find some secluded glade where she can pick wild flowers. And there, my faithful huntsman, you will kill her!"

"But Your Majesty, the little princess!"

"Silence! You know the penalty if you fail."

Knowing that he dare not disobey the Queen, the huntsman led Snow White into the forest. But when it came time for him to harm Snow White, he stopped and fell to his knees. "I can't do it. Forgive me Your Highness!"

"Why, why – I don't understand."

"The Queen is mad! She's jealous of you. She'll stop at nothing. Now quick, child – run, run away. Hide in the woods! Anywhere! And never come back!"

Frightened and alone, Snow White ran into the forest. Blazing eyes peered out at her from the darkness. Eerie shrieks pierced the air. The branches of trees grabbed at her. Finally she could run no farther and collapsed to the ground, sobbing.

When Snow White looked up, she saw several forest animals gathered around her.

"Hello. Do you know where I can stay? Maybe in the woods somewhere?"

Snow White followed the animals to a charming little cottage in the woods. She knocked on the door, but no one answered. So she went inside.

"Oh, it's adorable! Just like a doll's house. What a cute little chair. Why, there's seven little chairs. There must be seven little children. And by the looks of this table, seven untidy children. I know, I'll clean house and surprise them, then maybe they'll let me stay."

Suddenly, the dwarfs thought they heard a sound. Doc looked towards the stairs. "I-i-it's up there. In the bedroom."

Cautiously, the seven little men went to investigate. Doc slowly opened the door and peered in. "Why, i-i-it's a girl."

As the dwarfs approached the sleeping princess, she began to stir. "She's wakin' up! Hide!"

Doc dashed behind the beds, and the other dwarfs ran after him.

Snow White yawned and stretched. Then she noticed seven pairs of eyes looking at her over the end of beds. She sat up, smiling. "How do you do?"

"How do you do what?" Grumpy folded his arms, scowling.

Snow White laughed. "Let me guess. You must be Grumpy."

"Heh! I know who I am. Who are you?"

"Oh how silly of me. I'm Snow White."

"The princess?" Doc looked very impressed.

But Grumpy frowned. "Tell her to go back where she belongs."

Unable to make Snow White understand, the birds and animals raced to alert the dwarfs. At the mine, they pulled and tugged at the confused little men. Grumpy growled. "What ails these crazy critters? They ain't actin' this way for nothin'."

Doc thought about it. "Maybe it's – the Queen!"

Grumpy galloped off on the back of a deer. "Snow White's in danger! We've gotta save her!"

Meanwhile, the Queen picked up the poisoned apple. "Because you've been so good to poor old granny, I'll share a secret with you. This is no ordinary apple. It's a magic wishing apple!"

"A wishing apple, really?"

"Yes. One bite and all your dreams will come true."

The old woman grinned at the princess. "Perhaps there's someone you love?"

Snow White remembered her prince. "Well, there is someone."

"I thought so. Old Granny knows a young girl's heart. Now make a wish, and take a bite."

Snow White did so. "Oh, I feel strange."

A moment later, she fell to the ground.

A sudden storm began to rage as the dwarfs reached the cottage, where they found the lifeless Snow White. Through the rain, Grumpy spotted the old hag disappearing into the forest. "There she goes, men. After her!"

The dwarfs chased the Queen up a steep cliff. "You little fools. I'll crush yer bones!" She tried desperately to pry a boulder loose to crush them. Suddenly, a bolt of lightning shattered the ledge, sending the wicked Queen into the valley below.

Though the evil Queen was gone forever, the princess was still locked in her spell. So beautiful was she, even in death, the dwarfs could not find it in their hearts to bury her.

Doc brushed away a tear. "Let's make her a coffin out of glass and gold. That way, we can still see her and keep constant watch by her side."

The Prince heard of the beautiful maiden who slept in the glass coffin. He rode to the cottage of the seven dwarfs and they took him to Snow White. Gently, he kissed her. Then, slowly, her eyes began to open. The spell was broken. Love's first kiss had brought her back to life!

Snow White's wish finally came true. She bid the seven dwarfs goodbye as the handsome prince swept her into his arms.

Soon wedding bells rang, echoing throughout the forest. From then on, Snow White and her Prince Charming lived in their castle in the clouds ... happily ever after.